Oliver's Red Toboggan

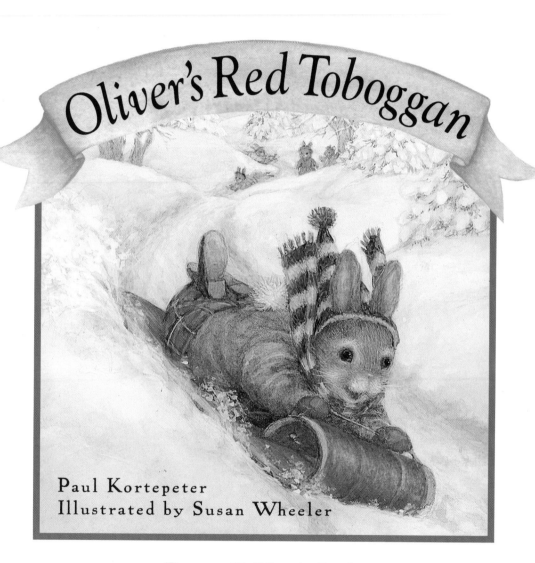

Paul Kortepeter
Illustrated by Susan Wheeler

Dutton Children's Books

All through the night the snow came down in great gusts. The creatures of Holly Pond Hill climbed under their blankets early and woke the next morning to a world as white as a wedding cake.

"Oh, please please pleeeease—let there be no school today!" Oliver Boxwood shouted, jumping up and down. "This is a snow-down-your-neck day, a play-till-your-toes-are-froze day! I'll finally get to try out my new red toboggan on Windy Hill."

"Will you let me try it, too?" asked his sister, Emily.

"Of course!" said Oliver. "Well . . . I'll *think* about it, anyway."

A bird fluttered down on the sill and tapped at the window.
It was the Morning News and Mail Bird. She sang:

"Bring skis, bring sleds—it's time to play.
School has been canceled for the day!"

"HOORAY!" yelled the two bunnies. They scrambled out of their pajamas and pulled on boots and coats and mittens.

Half a twinkling later, they were standing outside, breathing white clouds of frosty air.

"To WINDY HILL!" Emily shouted, and off they ran.

On the way, Oliver chattered excitedly about his brand–new
toboggan. "*My* toboggan will be the fastest ever seen!" he boasted.

They dashed past a tree house with its door ripped off and
climbed over a huge fallen branch. But Emily and Oliver did not
notice the damage the storm had brought. They were too eager to
go sledding.

When they got to Windy Hill, it was already zipping with sleds and skiers.

"I'll go down the first time," Oliver said, "since it's my toboggan."

"I'll go next time," said Emily. She watched Oliver flop on his belly and zing down the hill. She couldn't wait to try it.

"That was *great*!" said Oliver as he trudged up the hill toward Emily. "I want to go down again. After all, I've only used my new red toboggan once."

"Oh, okay," said Emily, rubbing her paws together to keep them warm. "But hurry up!" She watched enviously as he spun and slid down the slope, hooting with laughter.

Emily was very cross and her toes and whiskers felt frozen by the time Oliver reappeared.

"It's *my* turn now, Oliver," she said firmly.

But before she could grab the toboggan cord, Oliver scooted to the edge of the slope and went flying downhill again.

"You've been a *beast* to go down three times in a row!" she shouted at him when he came into view.

"Well, if you're going to call me names," Oliver said, "I won't let you use my toboggan at all." And with that, he sat down on the toboggan and sped away. Emily stomped off in the other direction.

All morning
long, Oliver had a
wonderful time.
The snow was soft
and sparkly, and he knew he
was the fastest bunny on the hill.

"Look at me, look at meeeeeeeee!" he yelled.

When Oliver began to feel hungry, he headed for home,
whistling as he went.

Suddenly he came upon a splendid castle made of snow.
At the top, Emily was standing guard.

"Wow, Emily," Oliver said. "Your castle is— GRANDNIFICENT."

"It is, isn't it?" she proudly replied.

"Mind if I come in?"

"As a matter of fact," Emily said majestically, "I *do* mind."

"I'll let you play with my toboggan."

"No, thank you." Emily yawned.

Oliver sat down in front of the castle.

"Well, I'm not leaving till you let me in," he said. Suddenly he was pelted with snowballs.

"I have plenty more ammunition where that came from," Emily warned.

Blobs of snow stuck to Oliver's ears, drooped from his whiskers, and dripped down his back. Oliver shivered, then ran all the way home. "I'll never let her use my toboggan— not *ever*!" he muttered.

Back at Boxwood Meadows, Emily and Oliver ate their lunch without saying a word to each other.

"Goodness!" exclaimed their mother. "You'd think you were having your teeth pulled instead of getting a day off from school. What's the matter?"

The whole story tumbled
out, with Emily telling her
side and Oliver telling his side
and both of them talking over
each other.

"Don't you remember that
little rhyme I used to say to
you two when you were
very small?" asked Victoria
Rose gently.

"*Sharing is a special
pleasure—share, share alike.
Giving makes for twice the
treasure—share, share alike.*"

"NEVER!" cried Emily
and Oliver, making faces at
each other.

After lunch, they hurried outside. Emily marched in the direction of her castle, and Oliver piled snowballs high on his toboggan. "Let's see how *she* likes being smacked with snow!" he whispered to himself.

When his toboggan was full, he pulled it to a hiding place behind a tree.

Oliver watched as Emily crouched down to examine a trail of tiny paw prints in the snow. The prints led right into her castle.

"Who's there?" she called, sounding a little nervous.

Several small, furry heads popped out of the window, and three figures appeared in the doorway. Emily stepped back in surprise. It was the squirrel family who lived near Windy Hill.

"Hello, Mr. Squirrel! Hello, Mrs. Squirrel! Hello, babies!" Oliver heard Emily say.

"Do you mind if we stay here
tonight?" Mr. Squirrel asked.
"The storm has badly damaged our tree house. It tore our
front door off its hinges, and it's not safe for our little ones to
stay there. If we line your wonderful castle with leaves, we'll
be cozy until we can find a new door."

"We won't stay long," Mrs. Squirrel promised.

Emily took a deep breath and patted the wall of her castle.
"You're welcome to stay as long as you like," she said.

Oliver caught up with Emily as she trudged home. "That was really nice of you."

Emily sighed. "Now I don't have a castle *or* a toboggan!"

"Well, if you can share your castle, I can share my toboggan," said Oliver. He gave his sister a friendly poke in the arm. "I have a really good idea."